Sky
the Blue
Fairy

For everyone who
believes in fairies

Special thanks to
Sue Bentley

No part of this publication may be reproduced
in whole or in part, or stored in a retrieval system, or
transmitted in any form or by any means, electronic,
mechanical, photocopying, recording, or otherwise,
without written permission of the publisher. For
information regarding permission, write to Working
Partners Limited, 1 Albion Place, London W6 OQT.

ISBN 0-439-69196-6

24 23 22 21   19 20 21 22

Printed in the U.S.A.

First Scholastic printing, February 2005

Sky the Blue Fairy

by Daisy Meadows

illustrated by Georgie Ripper

SCHOLASTIC INC.

New York   Toronto   London   Auckland   Sydney
Mexico City   New Delhi   Hong Kong   Buenos Aires

Cold winds blow and thick ice forms,
I conjure up this fairy storm.
To seven corners of the mortal world
the Rainbow Fairies will be hurled!

I curse every part of Fairyland,
with a frosty wave of my icy hand.
For now and always, from this fateful day,
Fairyland will be cold and gray!

Ruby, Amber, Sunny, and Fern
have been found. Now Rachel
and Kirsty must seek out
Sky the Blue Fairy

Contents

A Magic Messenger

"The water's really warm!" Rachel
Walker laughed. She was sitting on a
rock, swishing her toes in one of
Rainspell Island's deep blue rock pools.
Her friend Kirsty Tate was looking for
shells on the rocks nearby.

"Be careful you don't slip, Kirsty!"

called Mrs. Tate. She was sitting farther down the beach with Mrs. Walker.

"OK, Mom!" Kirsty yelled back. As she looked down at her bare feet, a patch of green seaweed began to move. There was something blue and shiny underneath it. "Rachel! Come over here," she shouted.

Rachel went over to Kirsty. "What is it?" she asked.

Kirsty pointed to the seaweed. "There's something blue under there," she said. "I wonder, could it be . . ."

"Sky the Blue Fairy?" Rachel said eagerly.

Jack Frost had banished the seven Rainbow Fairies from Fairyland with a magic spell. Now they were hidden on Rainspell Island. Until they were all found there would be no color in Fairyland. Rachel and Kirsty had promised the Fairy King and Queen to help find them.

The seaweed twitched.

Rachel felt her heart beat faster.

"Maybe the fairy is all tangled up," she whispered. "Like Fern when she landed on the ivy in the tower."

Fern was the Green Rainbow Fairy.
Rachel and Kirsty had already found
Fern and her sisters Ruby, Amber, and
Sunny.

Suddenly, a crab scuttled out from under
the seaweed. It was
bright blue and
very shiny.
Tiny rainbows
sparkled across
its shell. It didn't
look like any of
the other crabs on the beach.

Red
Orange
Yellow
Green
Blue
Indigo
Violet

Kirsty and Rachel smiled at each other.
This must be more of Rainspell Island's
special magic!

"Oh, no! Fairy in trouble!" the crab
muttered in a tiny voice. It sounded a bit
like two pebbles rubbing together.

4

"Did you hear that?" Rachel gasped.

The crab stopped and peered up at the girls with his little stalk eyes. Then he stood up on his back legs.

"What's he doing?" Kirsty said in surprise.

The crab pointed a claw toward some rocks farther along under the cliffs. He scuttled away for a few steps, then came back and looked up at Rachel and Kirsty again. "Over there," he said in his scratchy voice.

"I think he wants us to follow him," Rachel said.

"Yes! Yes!" said the little crab, clicking his claws. He set off sideways across a large, flat rock.

5

Kirsty turned to Rachel. "Maybe he knows where Sky is!"

"I hope so," Rachel replied, her eyes shining.

The crab scuttled across a stretch of sand. Rachel and Kirsty followed him. It was a hot, sunny day. Seagulls flew overhead on strong, white wings.

"Rachel, Kirsty, it's nearly lunchtime!" called Mrs. Walker. "We're going back to Dolphin Cottage."

Kirsty looked at Rachel in dismay. "But we have to stay here and look for the Blue Fairy. What will we do?"

The little crab jumped up and down, kicking up tiny puffs of sand. "Follow me, follow me!" he said.

Rachel thought quickly. "Mom?" she called back. "Could we have a picnic here instead, please?"

Mrs. Walker smiled. "Why not? It's a beautiful day. And we should make the most of the last three days of our vacation. I'll pop back to the cottage with Kirsty's mom and make some sandwiches."

Only three days, thought Kirsty, *and three*

Rainbow Fairies still to find: Sky, Inky, and Heather!

The two girls waved as their moms left. Kirsty turned to Rachel. "We'd better hurry. They'll be back soon."

The crab set off again over a big slippery rock. Rachel and Kirsty climbed carefully after him. Rachel saw him stop by a small pool. There were lots of pretty pink shells in it.

"Is the fairy in one of the rock pools?" she asked. "Is it this one?"

The crab
looked into
the pool. He
scratched the top
of his head with one
claw, looking puzzled.
Then he scuttled away.

"I guess not," Kirsty said.

"What about here?" Rachel said, stopping
by another pool. This
one had tiny silver
fish swimming in it.
But the crab
shook his claw
at them and
kept going.
"Not this
one, either,"
said Kirsty.

Suddenly, Rachel spotted a large pool.
It was all by itself, right at the foot of
the cliff. "Let's try that one," she said,
pointing.

Kirsty ran over.

The sky was reflected in the surface of
the pool like a shiny, blue mirror.

Rachel caught up with her friend. She
leaned over and looked into the water.

The crab scuttled up behind them, his stalk eyes wiggling like crazy. When he dipped his claw into the pool, the water fizzed like lemonade.

"Fairy!" cried the little crab, lifting his claw out of the water. Blue sparkles dripped off it and landed in the pool with a sizzle. The entire pool was shimmering with magic!

Bubble Trouble

"Thank you, little crab," Rachel said. She crouched down and stroked the top of the crab's shell.

The crab waved one claw at her, then dived into the water. He sank to the sandy bottom and scuttled out of sight under some seaweed.

Kirsty peered into the pool. "Can you see the Blue Fairy?" she asked.

Rachel shook her head.

Kirsty felt disappointed. "I can't, either."

"Do you think Jack Frost's goblins have found her?" Rachel said.

"I hope not!" Kirsty shuddered. "They'll do anything to stop the Rainbow Fairies from getting back to Fairyland."

Just then, Rachel and Kirsty heard a sweet voice singing a song. "With silver bells and cockle shells, and pretty maids all in a row . . ."

"Oh!" Rachel gasped. "Do you think it's the little crab?"

Kirsty shook her head. "His voice was all gritty."

"You're right," Rachel agreed. "This sounds tinkly — more like a fairy!"

"I think the singing is coming from that seaweed," said Kirsty, pointing into the rock pool.

Rachel peered right in. She could see something unusual in the rippling water. "Look!" she said.

A huge bubble came bobbing out of the seaweed. It floated toward the surface of the pool.

Rachel and Kirsty watched, their eyes very wide. There was a tiny girl inside the bubble! She waved at them and fluttered her rainbow-colored wings.

"Oh!" Kirsty gasped. "I think we've found Sky the Blue Fairy!"

The fairy pressed her hands against the curved sides of the bubble. She wore a short, sparkly dress and knee-high boots the color of bluebells. Her earrings and hairband were made of tiny stars.

"Please help me!" Sky said in a tiny voice that sounded like bubbles popping.

Suddenly, a cold breeze stirred Rachel's hair. A dark shadow fell across the pool. The glowing blue water turned gray. It was as if a cloud had covered the sun.

Rachel looked up. The sun was still shining brightly overhead. "What's happening?" she cried.

Kirsty heard a strange hissing, crackling sound. She glanced around in alarm.

A layer of frost was creeping across the rocks toward them, covering the beach in a crisp, white blanket.

"Jack Frost's goblins must be very near," Kirsty said, feeling worried.

In her bubble, Sky shivered, as ice began to cover the pool.

"Oh, no! She's going to be trapped," Kirsty cried.

Sky's bubble had stopped bobbing. Now it hung very still, frozen into the ice. Sky looked very scared.

"Poor Sky! We have to rescue her!" Rachel exclaimed. "But how can we melt all that ice?"

"I know!" said Kirsty. "Why don't we look in our magic bags?"

The Fairy Queen had given Rachel and Kirsty bags with very special gifts in them, to use for helping fairies in trouble.

"Of course!" Rachel said. Then she frowned. "Oh, no! I left them in my backpack on the other side of the rock pools!"

Goblins on Ice

"I'll run back and grab the magic bags,"
Rachel said, jumping quickly to her feet.

"OK," Kirsty said. She blew on her
hands to warm them. The frost was
making the air chilly. "I'll stay here. But
hurry!"

"I won't be long," Rachel promised. She

scrambled back over the rocks and onto
the sandy beach.

Her backpack was lying where she'd
left it. She reached inside and took out
one of the magic bags. It
was glowing with a
soft golden light.
When she opened
it, a cloud of glitter
sprayed out.
Rachel slipped
her hand into the
bag. There was
something there,
smooth and shiny
like a pebble. She
pulled it out and looked
closely at it. It was a tiny blue stone,
shaped a bit like a raindrop.

Rachel felt very puzzled. It was pretty, but how could it help?

Then the blue stone began to glow in her hand. It became hotter and hotter until it was almost too warm to hold. As it grew hotter, it glowed fiery red. Rachel curled her fingers around the raindrop stone in delight. They could use it to melt the ice and set Sky free!

She ran back as fast as she could. But when she reached the rocks, she stopped dead. Kirsty was still standing by Sky's frozen pool, but she wasn't alone anymore. Two ugly hook-nosed goblins were skating on the ice beside her!

"Shoo! Go away!" Kirsty was shouting at them, waving her hands.

Rachel could tell that Kirsty was really angry. Rachel didn't feel scared, now that she'd brought fairy magic to help fight the goblins.

"Go away yourself!" yelled one of the goblins rudely at Kirsty. He held his stumpy arms out sideways and slid across the ice on one foot away from her.

Kirsty tried to grab the other goblin.
But he dodged out of reach. "Can't
catch me!"

"Hee, hee! The fairy can't get out!" The
other goblin laughed. His bulging eyes
gleamed as he did a little twirl.

"We're *going* to get her out!" Kirsty
told him. "We're going to find *all* the
Rainbow Fairies. And then Fairyland will
get its colors back!"

"Oh no, it won't," said the goblin. He stuck out his tongue and screwed up his nose.

"Jack Frost's magic is too strong," said the other goblin. "Hey, look at me!" He pointed one foot out behind him and whizzed around the pool. But the ice was very slippery. He skidded sideways and crashed right into his friend.

Splat!

"Clumsy!" the goblin snapped angrily.

"You should have moved out of the way," grumbled the other one, rubbing his bottom.

The goblins tried to stand up. But their
feet skidded in all directions and they fell
over again in a heap. Rachel saw her
chance. She ran to the edge of the pool
and threw the magic blue stone onto
the ice.

Suddenly, there was a *fizz* and a *bang*!
A shower of golden sparks shot into the
air and the ice began to melt. A big hole
appeared in the center of the pool.

"Ow! Hot! Hot!" yelled the goblins,
slithering around on the ice. They
scrambled to the edge of the pool and
rushed away, their big feet slapping on
the rocks.

"They're gone!" Kirsty said in relief.

Rachel peered into the pool. "I hope
Sky isn't hurt," she said.

All the ice had melted and the water
reflected the blue sky once again. Sky's
bubble was floating just below
the surface.

Rachel saw Sky sit up inside the
bubble and look around. Her
eyes were big and scared,
and she looked very pale.

Kirsty put her hand in the water. It was still warm from the magic stone. "Don't be afraid, Sky," she said. Very gently, she poked her finger into the bubble.

Pop!

Sky tumbled free of the bubble and into the water. She swam up to the surface, her golden hair streaming behind her.

Kirsty leaned over and fished the fairy out. She felt like a tiny wet leaf. Kirsty placed her gently on a rock in the sun. "There you are, little fairy," she whispered.

Sky propped herself up on one elbow. Water dripped from her everywhere, but there were no blue sparkles now. "Thank you for helping me," she said in a weak voice.

Kirsty frowned at Rachel. "Something's wrong. All the fairies we found before had fairy dust. What has happened to Sky's sparkles?"

"I don't know," said Rachel. "And she's really pale, almost white."

It was true. Sky's dress was so pale, you could hardly tell it was blue at all.

Kirsty bit her lip. "It looks as if Jack Frost's magic has taken away her color!"

The blue crab scuttled out of the water and made his way across the rock to Sky. "Oh dear, oh dear," he muttered. "Poor little fairy."

Sky shivered and wrapped her arms around herself. "I'm so cold and sleepy," she whispered.

Kirsty felt a pang of alarm. "What's the matter, Sky? Did the goblins get too close to you?"

Sky nodded weakly. "Yes, and now I can't get warm."

"We've got to help her," Rachel said.

"But how?" asked Kirsty. She looked

down in dismay at Sky, curled up in a tiny ball with her eyes closed.

Rachel felt tears prick behind her eyelids.

Poor Sky. She looked really ill. What was going to happen to her?

Little Crab's Great Idea

Rachel spotted something moving. The little blue crab was wiggling his front claws wildly. "Look!" she said.

"He's trying to tell us something," said Kirsty.

The girls crouched down.

"Don't worry," the crab said in his gritty voice. "My friends will help us." He scuttled up to the top of the highest rock and snapped his claws.

"What's he going to do?" Kirsty wondered. Then she stared in amazement.

Lots and lots of crabs were coming out of the rock pools around them. Big ones, little ones, all different colors. Their claws made scratchy noises on the pebbles.

The blue crab wiggled his eyes and
clicked his claws, pointing up at the sky,
then down at the ground. His friends
pattered away in all directions. Their little
stalk eyes waved around as they prodded
their claws into the cracks between the
rocks.

Rachel and Kirsty looked at each
other, feeling very confused. "What's
going on?" said Rachel.

Just then, Kirsty spotted a tiny pink
crab tugging and tugging at something.
With a gritty crunch, the crab
tumbled over backward. It
held a fluffy white seagull
feather in its claws. The
crab scrambled up again,
waving the feather
in the air.
One by one, the other
crabs searched for more
feathers. Then the blue crab
waved them over to the rock where Sky
lay. Very carefully, he tucked the feathers
around the Blue Fairy. His friends
brought more and more feathers, until the
fairy was lying in a cozy feather bed.

"They're trying to warm Sky up with
seagull feathers!" Kirsty said.

Rachel held her breath. There were so
many feathers now that she couldn't see
the fairy at all. *Will the blue crab's idea
work?* she wondered.

There was the tiniest wriggle in the
feather nest. A faint puff of blue
sparkles fizzed up, smelling
of blueberries. One pale
blue star wobbled upward
and disappeared with a
pop.

"Fairy dust!" Rachel whispered.

"Mmmm . . . But there's not very much of it," Kirsty pointed out.

There was another wriggle from inside the nest. The feathers fell apart to reveal the Blue Fairy, her dress still very pale. She opened her big, blue eyes and sat up.

"Hello, I'm Sky the Blue Fairy. Who are you?" she said in a sleepy voice.

"I'm Kirsty," said Kirsty.

"And I'm Rachel," said Rachel.

"Thank you for frightening the goblins away," said Sky. "And thank you, little crab, for finding all these lovely, warm feathers." She tried to unfold her wings, but they were too crumpled. "My poor wings," said the fairy, her eyes filling with tiny tears.

"The feathers have helped, but Sky still can't fly," Kirsty said.

"Maybe the other Rainbow Fairies can help," Rachel said.

Sky looked up excitedly. "Do you know where my sisters are?" she asked.

"Oh, yes," said Kirsty. "So far, we've found Ruby, Amber, Sunny, and Fern."

"They are safe in the pot–at–the–end–
of–the–rainbow," Rachel added.

"Could you take me to them, please?"
said Sky. "I'm sure they will make me
better." She tried to stand up, but her legs
were too wobbly and she had to sit down
again.

"Here, let me carry you," Rachel offered.
She cupped her hands and scooped up the
feather nest with the fairy inside.

Sky waved at the little blue crab and
his friends. "Good-bye.
Thank you
again for
helping me."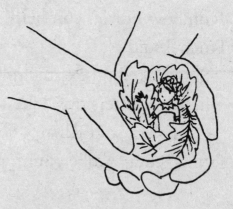

"Good-bye, good-bye!" The blue crab waved his claw. His friends waved, too, their little stalk eyes shining proudly. They had never rescued a Rainbow Fairy before.

Kirsty and Rachel glanced at each other as they crunched across the pebbles. Sky was being very brave, but the goblins had come closer to her than to any of the other Rainbow Fairies. And now the Blue Fairy was hardly blue at all!

Back to the Pot!

Rachel and Kirsty hurried across the fields and into the woods. Rachel carried Sky very carefully. The fairy lay curled in a ball in the warm feathers, her cheek resting on her pale hands.

"Here's the glade with the willow tree," Kirsty said.

The scent of oranges hung in the air, tickling their noses. Rachel looked around and spotted a tiny fairy. She was hovering over a patch of daisies, collecting nectar in an acorn cup.

"Look!" Rachel said. "It's Amber the Orange Fairy."

"Hello again, Rachel and Kirsty!" Amber fluttered over and settled on Rachel's shoulder.

Then Amber saw Sky lying curled up in Rachel's hand. "Oh, no! Sky, what happened? I must call the others," she cried. She waved her wand and a fountain of sparkling orange dust shot into the air.

The other Rainbow Fairies fluttered up
all over the clearing. The air sparkled
with red, orange, yellow, and green fairy
dust. Bubbles and flowers, tiny butterflies
and leaves sprinkled the grass.

Rachel and Kirsty watched as the
fairies clustered around Sky. The Blue
Fairy sat up slightly and gave a weak
smile, then flopped back into her nest of
feathers.

"Oh, Sky!" cried Fern, the gentle Green Fairy.

"Why is she so pale?" Sunny asked.

"The goblins got really close to her," Rachel explained. "They froze the pond. Sky was trapped in a bubble under the ice."

"Oooh! That's terrible." Sunny shuddered.

"Kirsty shouted at them and tried to catch them," Sky whispered.

"Thank you. You are so brave!" said Ruby the Red Fairy, then she zoomed high into the air.

"We must think of something to help Sky! Oh, I know! Let's ask Bertram for his advice!"

The fairy sisters sped toward the willow tree, their wings flashing brightly. Rachel and Kirsty carried Sky over in her feathery nest.

The pot-at-the-end-of-the-rainbow lay on its side underneath the willow's trailing branches. The Rainbow Fairies were living there until all their sisters had been found and they could go back to Fairyland.

As Rachel put Sky down beside the pot, a large green frog hopped out.

"Miss Sky!" he croaked, looking pleased.

"Hello, Bertram." Sky gave another weak smile.

"We have to make Sky warm so she gets her color back," Fern explained.

Bertram looked very worried. "Jack Frost's goblins are so cruel," he said. "You all must stay close to the pot so that I can protect you."

"Don't worry," said Sunny, giving Sky a hug. "You'll feel better soon."

Sky nodded, but she didn't answer. Her eyes started to close. She was so pale, her arms and legs seemed almost transparent.

Rachel and Kirsty watched the Rainbow Fairies exchange worried glances. "Oh, Bertram, what if the goblins have hurt Sky forever!" exclaimed Fern. "What can we do to save her?"

The Fairy Ring

Bertram looked very serious. "I think it's time for you all to try a spell."

Amber frowned. "It might not work with only four of us. Rainbow Magic needs seven fairies!"

"Bertram's right, we have to try," Ruby said. "Maybe we can manage a *small* spell. Quick, let's make a fairy ring."

The Rainbow Fairies fluttered into a circle above Sky.

Rachel noticed a black-and-yellow queen bee and a small gray squirrel appear at the edge of the glade. "Queenie and Fluffy have come to watch the spell," she whispered to Kirsty. Queenie the bee had helped Sunny get her wand back after the goblins stole it. Fluffy the squirrel had carried Fern and the girls back to

the pot when the goblins were chasing them. "Ready, sisters!" said Ruby. She lifted her wand. *"In a fairy ring we fly, to bring blue color back to Sky!"* she chanted. The other fairies waved their wands. Four different colors of fairy dust sparkled in the air — red, orange, yellow, and green. The dust covered Sky in a glittering multi-colored cloud as she lay in the nest of feathers on the soft, green grass.

"Something's happening!" Kirsty said. Through the cloud of dust, she could see that Sky's short dress and knee-high boots were turning bluer and bluer. "The spell is working!"

Whoosh!

A shimmering cloud of blue stars shot into the air. They drifted up to the sky, where they faded away with tiny *pops*.

"We did it!" cheered Amber, turning a cartwheel in the air, as Sunny clapped her hands in delight.

"Hooray for Rainbow Magic!" shouted Ruby.

Sky yawned and sat up. She brushed the feathers away and looked down at herself. Her face lit up. Her dress was blue again! "My wings feel strong enough to fly now," she said. She flapped them twice, then zoomed into the air. She did a twirl, her wings flashing with rainbows.

"Thank you, sisters!"

The Rainbow Fairies clustered around
Sky, hugging and kissing her. The air
around them bubbled with fairy dust —
red, orange, yellow, green, and blue. It was
nearly a whole rainbow!

Rachel and Kirsty beamed.

Fern swooped down and scooped up an
armful of seagull feathers. "You won't
need these anymore!" She
laughed, tickling Sky with a
long, white one.

"But I think I might know what to
do with them!" said Sky. She flew
down to perch on the edge of the pot
and peeked in. "It's so cozy!" she said,
admiring the tiny chairs and tables
made of twigs and the giant shell bed.

Then Sky fluttered over to the rest of
the feathers and gathered them up. "I
thought we could put these on our bed.
They'll be very warm and soft."

Her fairy sisters looked delighted.
"Thanks, Sky. What a good idea," said
Ruby.

"Let's have a welcome-home feast," said
Fern. "With wild strawberries and clover
juice."

Amber did another cartwheel.

"Yippee! Rachel and Kirsty, you're
invited, too!"

"Thank you, but we have to go."
Rachel looked at her watch. "Our moms
will be waiting with our picnic."

"Oh, yes!" Kirsty remembered, jumping
up. She felt a bit disappointed that she
wouldn't have a chance to taste some
fairy food. But she didn't want her mom
to be worried. "Good-bye, we'll be back
again soon!"

The fairies sat on the edge of the pot
and waved to the girls. Queenie, Fluffy,
and Bertram the Frog waved, too. "Good-
bye! Good-bye!"

Sky fluttered beside Rachel and Kirsty as they walked back across the glade. Tiny rainbows sparkled on her wings. Her dress and boots glowed bright blue, and blueberry scent filled the air.

"Thank you so much, Rachel and Kirsty," she said. "Now five Rainbow Fairies are safe."

"We'll find Inky and Heather, too," Kirsty said. "I promise."

"Yes," Rachel agreed.

As they made their way back to the beach, Rachel looked at Kirsty. "Do you think we can find them in time? We only have two days of vacation left. And the goblins are getting much closer. They nearly caught Sky today!"

Kirsty squeezed her friend's hand and smiled. "Don't worry. Nothing is going to stop us from keeping our promise to the Rainbow Fairies!"

RAINBOW magic

Ruby, Amber, Sunny, Fern,
and Sky are safe at last.
But where is
Inky the Indigo Fairy?

A Fairytale Beginning

"Rain, rain, go away." Rachel Walker sighed. "Come again another day!"

She and her friend Kirsty Tate stared out of the attic window. Raindrops splashed against the glass, and the sky was full of purplish-black clouds.

"Isn't it a horrible day?" Kirsty said. "But it's nice and cozy in here."

She looked around Rachel's small attic bedroom. There was just enough room for a brass bed with a patchwork quilt, a comfy armchair, and an old bookcase.

"You know what the weather on Rainspell is like," Rachel pointed out. "It might be hot and sunny very soon!"

Both girls had come to Rainspell Island on vacation. The Walkers were staying in Mermaid Cottage, while the Tates were in Dolphin Cottage next door.

Kirsty frowned. "Yes, but what about Inky the Indigo Fairy?" she asked. "We have to find her today."

Rachel and Kirsty shared a wonderful secret. They were trying to find the seven Rainbow Fairies who had been cast out of Fairyland by evil Jack Frost. Fairyland would be cold and gray until all seven fairies had been found again.

Rachel thought of Ruby, Amber, Sunny, Fern, and Sky, who were all safe now in the pot-at-the-end-of-the-rainbow. They had only Inky the Indigo Fairy and Heather the Violet Fairy left to find. But how could they look for them while they were stuck indoors?

"Remember what the Fairy Queen said?" she reminded Kirsty.

Kirsty nodded. "She said the magic would come to us." Suddenly, she looked scared. "Maybe the rain is Jack Frost's magic. Maybe he's trying to stop us from finding Inky."

"Oh, no!" Rachel said. "Let's hope it stops soon. But what will we do while we're waiting?"

Kirsty thought for a moment. Then she went over to the bookcase. It was filled with dusty, old books, and she pulled one out. It was so big, she had to use two hands to hold it.

"*The Big Book of Fairy Tales,*" Rachel read out, looking at the cover.

"If we can't find fairies, at least we can read about them!" Kirsty grinned.

The two girls sat down on the bed and put the book on their knees. Kirsty was about to turn the first page when Rachel gasped. "Kirsty, look at the cover! It's purple. A really deep purplish-blue."

"That's indigo," Kirsty whispered. "Oh, Rachel! Do you think Inky could be trapped inside?"

"Let's see," Rachel said. "Hurry up, Kirsty. Open the book!"

But Kirsty had spotted something else. "Rachel," she said shakily. "It's *glowing*."

Rachel looked. Kirsty was right. Some pages in the middle of the book were gleaming with a soft purplish-blue light.

Kirsty opened the book. The ink on the pages was glowing indigo. For a moment, Kirsty thought that Inky might fly out of the pages, but there was no sign of her. On the first page was a picture of a wooden soldier. Above the picture were the words: *The Nutcracker.*

"Oh!" Rachel said. "I know this story. I went to see the ballet at Christmas."

"What's it about?" Kirsty asked.

"Well, a girl named Clara gets a wooden nutcracker soldier for Christmas," Rachel explained. "He comes

to life and takes her to the Land of Sweets." They looked down at a brightly colored picture of a Christmas tree. A little girl was asleep beside it, holding a wooden soldier.

On the next page there was a picture of snowflakes whirling and swirling through a dark forest. "Aren't the pictures great?" Kirsty said. "The snow looks so real."

Rachel frowned. For a moment, she thought the snowflakes were moving. Gently she put out her hand and touched the page. It felt cold and wet!

"Kirsty," she whispered. "It *is* real!" She held out her hand. There were white snowflakes on her fingers.

Kirsty looked down at the book again, her eyes wide. The snowflakes started to swirl from the book's pages, right into the bedroom, slowly at first, then faster and faster.

Read the rest of

RAINBOW magic

Inky the Indigo Fairy

to find out what magic the swirling snowstorm brings with it.